GW00454898

by Melanie Joyce
Illustrated by David Shephard

Titles in Ignite

Alien Sports TV	Jonny Zucker
Monster Diner	Danny Pearson
Team Games	Melanie Joyce
Mutant Baby Werewolf	Richard Taylor
Rocket Dog	Lynda Gore
The Old Lift	Alison Hawes
Spiders from Space	Stan Cullimore
Gone Viral	Mike Gould
The Ghost Train	Roger Hurn
Dog Diaries	Clare Lawrence

Badger Publishing Limited
Oldmedow Road, Hardwick Industrial Estate,
King's Lynn PE30 4JJ
Telephone: 01438 791037

www.badgerlearning.co.uk

Team Games ISBN 978 1 84926 955 1

First edition © 2012
This second edition © 2014

Text © Melanie Joyce 2012
Complete work © Badger Publishing Limited 2012

Publisher: Susan Ross
Senior Editor: Danny Pearson
Designer: Fiona Grant
Illustrator: David Shephard

Contents

Vocabulary:

trouble   impressed

embarrassed   horribly

hugged   trainers

Main characters:

Sheena

Chapter 1

Trouble

Sunday February 20th, 6 p.m.
I am Sheena Kendra and I am in trouble again. Mum says it has to stop.

"Work hard and do your homework," she says. "Stop getting into trouble."

Mum says I should join the school sports team.

"Sport will keep you out of trouble," she says. I am not so sure.

Monday February 21st, 5.30 p.m.
Today I asked Coach Briggs if I could join the sports team. He didn't look impressed. "Try the javelin," he said.

I ran across the field. I ran so fast, I tripped and let go of the javelin.

It flew right past Coach Briggs's ear. "Try the discus," he said.

The discus was a disaster. "Swing it round and let go," said Coach Briggs.

I swung so much I got dizzy. I let go of the discus.

"Duck!" shouted a voice. SMASH!
The discus flew right through the
science lab window.

Why can't I stay out of trouble?

Tuesday February 22nd, 6 p.m.
Everyone at school knows I smashed
the science lab window. When I walk
past them, they duck and laugh.
I don't want to be laughed at.

I don't want to be the girl that
everyone looks at and just sees trouble.
If only I could find something I'm good
at doing.

Monday February 28th, 7 p.m.

I tried the long jump today. When I jumped, I threw my legs forward, but skidded onto my bottom instead of landing on my heels.

I tore a large hole in my tracksuit bottoms. Everyone was too shocked to laugh.

I have never been so embarrassed in my life. Why do I fail at everything?

CHAPTER 2
Try again

Thursday March 3rd, 7.15 p.m.
Today Coach Briggs said I should try
the hurdles. Things didn't go well.

A wasp flew into my face.
I waved my arms as if
I was on fire. I crashed
into the hurdles.
It was a disaster.

I am running out of things
to try.

Thursday March 10th, 6.20 p.m.

Mum asked me why I was upset today.

"Because I keep failing," I said.

Mum said I should keep trying. She said
that nothing good comes without
effort. But what if the effort doesn't
pay off? What is the point of trying
when all I do is fail?

Monday March 14th, 7.25 p.m.

I am the school joke. If they needed a clown on the sports team, it would be me.

Trying the pole vault was my last chance. It all went horribly wrong.

I landed on Coach Briggs. He couldn't speak. He didn't need to speak.

The look on his face said it all.

I am finished with sport. Mum was wrong. It isn't going to keep me out of trouble.

I get into trouble because that's the only thing I'm good at doing. I'm no good at anything else.

People laugh at me because I am a joke. I feel like such a loser.

CHAPTER 3

On your marks

Friday April 1st, 5 p.m.
Everything has changed. Something amazing happened today.

I was at the bus stop. Across the road, I saw a woman with a little boy on a tricycle.

She was talking to her friend. She did not see the little boy ride away. He rode down the hill.

It all happened so quickly. The wheels on the bike went faster and faster.

The little boy cried out. His mother cried out. I dropped my school bag.

I checked the road for cars and I ran. I ran down that hill as fast as I could.

Had Mum put extra vitamins in my porridge? Had I turned into a super hero? I don't know, but I stopped the tricycle.

Everyone cheered. The boy's mum hugged me. My friends couldn't believe it. "You can run so fast!" they said.

No one at school is laughing at me now.

They think I'm a hero. At last, I have found something I am good at doing.

I can run. I am going to see Coach Briggs tomorrow.

I'll show him I'm good at something. This time I won't fail.

CHAPTER 4

The relay

Saturday April 2nd, 3.30 p.m.
I did it! I'm on the relay team. Today,
I met my teammates Elsa, Carey and
Deb. They were really nice.

They told me the training would be
tough. "It's tough but it's worth it,"
they said. "You'll need good trainers,"
they said.

Mum can't afford new trainers.

Wednesday April 13th, 5.30 a.m.
The training is tough. I get up early, I run every day.

My times are getting faster. Coach Briggs says I could make the team for the National Athletic Championships.

The trials are on Saturday. I hope my trainers don't fall apart before then.

Saturday April 16th, 7.15 p.m.

The trials were held today. "You'll be OK," said Deb. "Just do your best."

I felt so scared. My stomach was churning. I was first to run.

I had to give it my best shot. Before I knew it, the buzzer had gone. I kicked off quickly.

The other runners pushed ahead.
I passed the baton to Carey. She raced ahead.

Carey passed the baton to Elsa. Elsa ran and passed to Deb. "Run, Deb, run!" I cried. Deb ran like the wind.

She was first over the line. We were through to the championships!

CHAPTER 5

Pure gold

Monday April 18th, 6.15 p.m.
Coach Briggs told Mum I had to have
proper trainers.

When I got up this morning, I couldn't
find my old trainers. "Where are they?"
I asked Mum.

"In the bin," she replied.

I nearly had a heart attack.

Then mum showed me the box.
"Open it," she said.

I opened the box.

Inside was a pair of red Cobra trainers. They must have cost a fortune.

"I've been saving up," said Mum.

I hugged her. I was finally ready for the championships.

Saturday May 28th

Today, we went to the National Athletic Championships.

I will remember it forever. There were teams from all over the country.

The stadium was packed. It felt electric.

"Warm up," said Coach Briggs. "It's time to run."

All the training paid off. We outran the teams in the heats. We made it to the final.

But Deb pushed too hard to win. She pulled a muscle.

Coach Briggs said I had to be the anchor runner in the final. I was so nervous my legs shook.

The buzzer went. Deb was running first.

The pulled muscle was slowing her down.

She passed to Carey, who belted round the bend. She passed to Elsa, but we were behind.

We were losing in the final.

Suddenly, I could see Elsa charging towards me.

I held out my hand. The baton landed with a smack. I was off.

I could see the heels of the other runners. I had to catch them. I thought of Mum. I thought of how my life had been. I wasn't going back there.

I had everything to run for.

Suddenly, I was over the line.

The crowd roared. My heart pounded in my chest. Hands patted my back.

"Well done," they said. What did they mean? I saw Mum in the crowd. She was crying. But why?

Elsa, Carey and Deb ran up. They hugged me. "We won!" they cried.

It was the best moment of my life.

It was not because we came first, either.

It was because we were a team. It was because, at last, something good had happened. I made it happen by working hard.

Super sports

One of the greatest sporting events in the world is the Olympic Games. It brings together countries from all over the world to compete for gold, silver and bronze medals.

The origins of the Olympics are in Ancient Greece. Thought to have been staged in honour of the god Zeus, the first recorded games were held in 776 BC in Olympia.

Around 900 BC, the first gymnasiums were created by Greek athletes, who practised naked to music.

The modern Olympic Games were first held in 1896 in Athens, Greece. There were 311 competitors, all of whom were male.

Women were not allowed to compete in the modern Olympics until 1900.

Modern additions to the original Olympic summer sports are the Winter Olympics, Paralympics and Youth Olympic Games.

So far, Norway has won the most medals in the Winter Games. To date, the United States has won the most medals in the Summer Games.

The Olympics is symbolised by five rings. Each ring represents a region of the world: Africa, the Americas, Asia, Europe, and Oceania.

Any country that wishes to host the Games must first submit an application to the International Olympic Committee.

The modern Olympics feature over 17,000 athletes from 205 countries. Each of those athletes is focused on one thing, and one thing alone – the glory of Olympic gold!

Questions

Why is Sheena unhappy at the beginning of the story?

Who tells Sheena to join the sports team?

What is the name of the sports coach?

Can you name the first sport that Sheena tries?

How does the science lab window get broken?

How does Sheena find out that she can run fast?

What team does Sheena join?

Which teammate injures herself in a race?

What does Sheena's mum buy for her?

Why is Sheena happy in the end?